SUPPORT

LOVE

Para Andrea,

La Belleza mas
importante viene de el
corazón. Siempre Sé tu misma.
Te quiero!
Ani

To Danny and Jack who fill my heart with so much love and happiness. Thank you for putting the color inside of my world.

- Ana

To my family whose support and love make it all worthwhile.

- J.R.

**www.mascotbooks.com**

*Little Monkey, Be You*

©2015 Ana Harris. All Rights Reserved. No part of this publication may be reproduced, stored in a retrieval system or transmitted in any form by any means electronic, mechanical, or photocopying, recording or otherwise without the permission of the author.

Puzzle pieces art by Michael Marquez

**For more information, please contact:**
Mascot Books
560 Herndon Parkway #120
Herndon, VA 20170
info@mascotbooks.com

Library of Congress Control Number: 2014921193

CPSIA Code: PRT0415A
ISBN-13: 978-1-62086-909-3

Printed in the United States

# Little Monkey, Be You

Written by **Ana Harris**
Illustrations by **Joe Ruiz**

One day, a little monkey was born. He had ten little fingers and ten teeny-tiny toes. He was quite small but was perfect. His mom and dad named him Max and loved him more than anything.

Max started to grow bigger and bigger until he was not so little anymore. His parents knew he was very special. He was different from other monkeys. He didn't look different, but he acted a little different sometimes. Everyone who really knew Max loved him for who he was.

Max loved to run, jump, and swing upside down. He had lots of energy. He didn't like a change in his routine though, it would scare him. But things were about to change because he was starting school!

"It's your first day of school!" said his mom as she woke up Max.

But Max did not want to go. He threw himself on the floor and started kicking and screaming,

His mom picked him up to try and comfort him. Then, all of a sudden, Max arched his back so far that his mom lost her balance and fell. *Oh no! I'm sorry, Mommy,* thought Max, looking worried. He didn't mean to do that.

"Max," said his mom, "sometimes things change in life. It will take a little getting used to, but everything will fall into place like the pieces of a puzzle. It is important that you at least try. Just be yourself. Little monkey, be you."

So Max got ready for school, with Mom's help of course.

When he came downstairs, his favorite breakfast was waiting. Banana pancakes, "Mmmm, yummy." Then, he was off to school.

When Max got to his new classroom, his teacher, Ms. Fox, was there to greet everyone. Max looked around. There were so many colorful toys and books. *Wow*, thought Max. He was excited!

Finally, all the parents had to say goodbye. Ms. Fox told all the kids to sit in a circle. Max didn't want to, so he just stood. She asked everyone's name, going one by one in the circle. When she got to Max, he didn't answer and looked away.

Max was thinking. Plus, he was still a little nervous. Just when he was about to answer, Ms. Fox moved on to a rhino sitting next to him. Sometimes Max just needed a little more time to think things through.

During playtime, all the animals rushed to the toys. One small turtle fell, so Max stopped and helped him get back up. He started to play with the cars. Max lined all the cars up into one long row. It took him almost all of playtime to do this.

Max stopped and looked at his cars. He smiled with pride.

Then, a bear named Elmi started to kick all of the cars out of order.

Max got so angry, he started crying and ran out of the classroom.

The next day at lunchtime, Max was looking for a seat. He sat on a bench near some other animals in his class. Elmi came over and said, "You are always lining the cars up in class, and you don't talk to anyone. You are weird! Go away."

Tears filled Max's eyes, but he tried hard not to cry. He walked away and sat under a tree. He opened up his lunchbox and saw a letter from his mom. It said: *You are so special. I love you more today than I loved you yesterday. There is no limit to my love.*

Max felt happy. He knew his mom loved him no matter what.

Max noticed a zebra named Zoey didn't have lunch. He looked down at the other half of his sandwich, then walked over to Zoey and gave it to her. He smiled and walked away as she thanked him.

During recess, some kids were playing hide-and-go-seek. Max tried to join in on the fun. The kids started to run away laughing. Elmi was leading the group. Max knew he was a bully. His feelings were hurt.

Max went home frustrated.

"How did school go?" his dad asked.

Max didn't answer him.
When his dad asked again,
Max's eyes welled up with tears.

"Oh, buddy, what happened?"

Max finally asked, "Am I weird?"

"Absolutely not! You are perfect just the way you are. Yes, you are different. Sometimes change overwhelms you. Sometimes you do not speak to express yourself. You like things in a specific order, but these are the things that make you unique. Being different is special. If everyone were the same, life would be boring."

Max smiled. His dad always knew what to say to make him feel better.

A few days later, all the kids were playing at the playground. There was lots of laughter and smiles. Max noticed a fox named Marcos had part of his shirt stuck on the slide. Max helped loosen his shirt so he could pass. They smiled at each other and continued to play.

Max climbed to the top of the playground. He hung upside down and started to swing. "Wee! Wee!" said Max.

All of a sudden, Elmi walked up to Max and said, "You're a weirdo!" Elmi and some of the other animals started to laugh.

Ms. Fox overheard. She looked at Elmi. "Do not call anyone names! Everyone is special in their own, unique way. Don't be a bully, Elmi. Be a buddy."

Elmi looked embarrassed and ran off.

When Max was having dinner that night,
his mom asked how school was going.

Max said, "I have no friends. This bear in class told me
I was a weirdo," and he looked very sad.

Mom and Dad looked at each other. Mom said, "You are not a weirdo. I love you just the way you are. Continue to be yourself and real friends will see how great you are. Little monkey, be you. You were born to be awesome." She winked at Max.

Max felt good about himself. He felt loved.

The very next morning Max was getting ready for school,
but he didn't feel like going. Then he remembered those
words: Little monkey, be you.

Max had an idea. He got to school really early and started working on his masterpiece. Little did anyone know, Max was a block-building pro. He could stack blocks like nobody else. He built a tunnel out of blocks complete with a limbo stick!

As the other animals started to get to class, they were very impressed. They were smiling. "Wow, Max! That is so cool!" said one little tiger.

Max smiled and said, "Thank you!"

Ms. Fox knew that Max was having a hard time making friends. She looked at his amazing creation and turned on the music.

♪ Dance block party! ♫

All the kids started laughing, dancing, and taking turns doing the limbo.

Elmi walked over to Max and said, "I'm sorry for being mean to you and calling you names. I was wrong and didn't realize how fun you are."

"I forgive you, Elmi."

They smiled and continued to dance. Everyone had a great time.

Later at lunch, Marcos and Zoey sat with Max. Max did not realize it before, but when he showed Zoey and Marcos kindness they had become his friends.

Max had another note in his lunchbox that read: *I love you more today than I loved you yesterday. My love has no limit.* He smiled and felt a lot of joy in his heart.

At bedtime, Max sat on his dad's lap and told him about his great day. Max started to flap his hands with excitement. "Daddy, how did you know everything was going to fall into place?"

"I knew everything would work out as long as you were true to yourself. You can do anything you want to do. Don't ever be afraid to be yourself. I look at you and I see all the pieces of my heart. I see you, and you are perfect. Little monkey, be you!"

## About the Author

Ana Harris lives in Florida with her loving husband and two energetic and adorable little boys. Writing has always been a passion and having children of her own sparked a newfound interest in children's books. She has always believed children should know the importance of being themselves, to be confident in who they are, and to feel loved.

## Have a book idea?

**Contact us at:**

Mascot Books

560 Herndon Parkway

Suite 120

Herndon, VA

**info@mascotbooks.com | www.mascotbooks.com**

HOPE

AWARENESS